Big Thunder Magic

by Craig Kee Strete

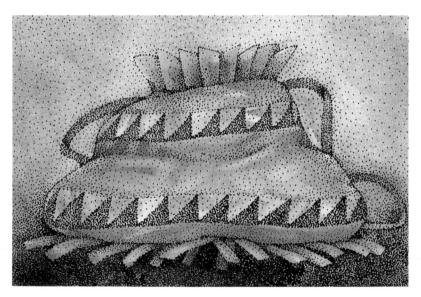

pictures by Craig Brown

GREENWILLOW BOOKS  NEW YORK

Pen-and-ink and pastels were used for the full-color art.
The text type is ITC Cheltenham Book.

Text copyright © 1990 by Craig Kee Strete
Illustrations copyright © 1990 by Craig McFarland Brown
All rights reserved. No part of this book
may be reproduced or utilized in any form
or by any means, electronic or mechanical,
including photocopying, recording, or by
any information storage and retrieval
system, without permission in writing
from the Publisher, Greenwillow Books,
a division of William Morrow & Company, Inc.,
105 Madison Avenue, New York, NY 10016.
Printed in Singapore by Tien Wah Press
First Edition   10 9 8 7 6 5 4 3 2 1

Library of Congress Cataloging-in-Publication Data

Strete, Craig Kee.
Big thunder magic / by Craig Kee Strete ;
pictures by Craig Brown.
p.   cm.
Summary: Relates how Thunderspirit, a very small and timid ghost,
manages to rescue his friend Nanabee the sheep from the zoo.
ISBN 0-688-08853-8. ISBN 0-688-08854-6 (lib. bdg.)
[1. Ghosts—Fiction.   2. Sheep—Fiction.
3. Friendship—Fiction.   4. Pueblo Indians—Fiction.
5. Indians of North America—Fiction.]
I. Brown, Craig McFarland, ill.   II. Title.
PZ7.S9164Bi   1990   [E]—dc20   89-34613   CIP   AC

TO LINDA,

WITH LOVE AND DREAMS

—C.B.

In a quiet Pueblo near the edge of the great desert lived two good friends.

There was Nanabee the sheep and Thunderspirit, who despite his scary name was a very small, very timid ghost. When the sun went down, Thunderspirit crept through the Pueblo. He made the sounds of ghost wind and ghost thunder. When the people heard Thunderspirit, they knew day was done and that it was time to sleep.

And when Thunderspirit walked, Nanabee the sheep would run and look in the corners of the Pueblo rooms to see if there were any stray bunches of grass that she might eat. Just before sleep, a little bit of dried grass tasted very good. Then Nanabee would move to her favorite sleeping place close to the night fire.

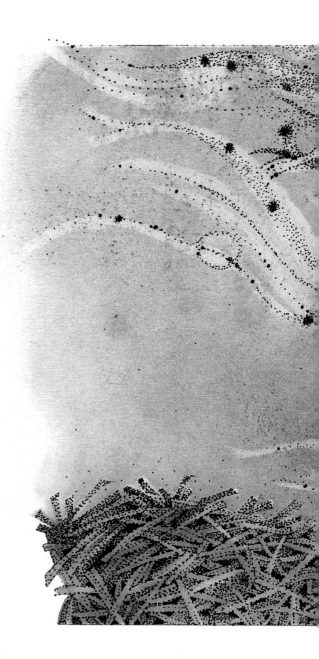

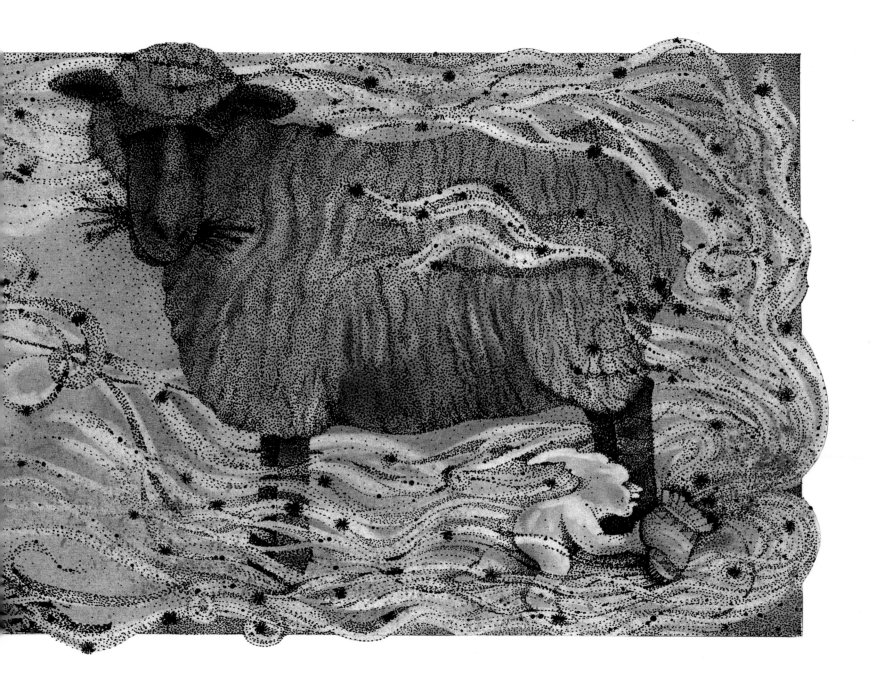

When Thunderspirit walked at night and made his ghost noises, then the Great Chief was happy. When he heard those sounds, he knew good spirits were in his Pueblo, and he closed his eyes and slept peacefully.

When all the people in the Pueblo were asleep, Thunderspirit would come back shivering with the cold and lie down beside his warm friend Nanabee the sheep.

So life went in the Pueblo. But one day the Great Chief decided to go to the city, and he took Nanabee the sheep with him.

Thunderspirit had grown so used to sleeping next to his friend Nanabee that he couldn't sleep that night! Without Nanabee's soft, warm coat to lie next to, Thunderspirit turned as blue as the sky!

So Thunderspirit put his magic medicine bag full of thunder sounds on his back and went to the city to find his friend. It was a very long walk to the city!

Thunderspirit followed the Great Chief and Nanabee into the center of the city.

The Chief went to find a place to stay. He went to a hotel.

He asked for a room with grass for Nanabee the sheep.

But the people in the hotel did not understand. They said

they did not rent rooms to sheep.

The Chief said Nanabee did not want to rent a room.

He said Nanabee doesn't have any money. He said,

"I am the one that wants to rent the room.

I have the money."

They told him to go sleep in the park.

So he did.

It was the time of night when Thunderspirit made his ghost sounds.

He took thunder sounds out of his magic medicine bag and threw them up high in the air. But the sound of a taxi honking its horn was louder.

He took a ghost wind sound out of his bag and threw it up high in the air. But a train went by. The sound of its wheels was louder.

Thunderspirit decided the city was not a good place for thunder magic. It was not a good place for ghost wind magic.

So he put his magic things back in his bag and went to find Nanabee. It was very cold. Thunderspirit had walked a very long way. He wanted to sleep beside his warm friend Nanabee.

The ground in the park was hard, so the Chief did not sleep
very well. But it did not cost anything to sleep in the park.
The Chief liked that.
There was lots of green grass, so Nanabee was very happy.
She wandered off, eating that good-tasting grass.
Thunderspirit found the Chief asleep in the park.

Everything would have been fine, but the sun was coming up, and people began to notice Nanabee eating grass in the park! A papergirl on her bike saw Nanabee first. She told a milkman. The milkman told a street sweeper.

The street sweeper worked for the city, and he said, "Sheep are not allowed in the park! The grass in the park is for people! Sheep aren't supposed to eat it!"

The street sweeper called a police officer.

The police officer said, "I only arrest people. Sheep are not people." The police officer called a fire fighter.

The fire fighter said, "I only put out fires. This sheep is not on fire." The fire fighter called a dogcatcher.

The dogcatcher said, "I only catch dogs. A sheep is not a dog." The dogcatcher called a zookeeper.

The zookeeper went out to the park. He saw Nanabee eating grass. He said, "It is very unusual to see a sheep eating grass in a city park. This must be a very unusual sheep."

And because Nanabee was such an unusual animal, he took Nanabee to the zoo in a big truck.

Ghosts see many things, and Thunderspirit saw it all.

Thunderspirit went to rescue Nanabee.

He took a taxi. He didn't have any money, but he was a
very small ghost, so he could ride on top. The taxi driver
didn't even know Thunderspirit was up there!

At the zoo Thunderspirit saw animals everywhere, but he didn't see Nanabee. He heard a lion sound, an elephant sound, and a monkey sound. Then he heard a sad little sound that sounded like this:

Baaaaaaa!

He knew that was a Nanabee sound!

And there on the bottom of a cage was poor Nanabee, dreaming about green grass and Indian land without cages. What a sad thing it was to see Nanabee there!

The door of the cage was locked with a big iron lock.

Thunderspirit did not have a key.

But he still had a little magic left.

Thunderspirit opened his magic medicine bag and
put it up against the iron lock.

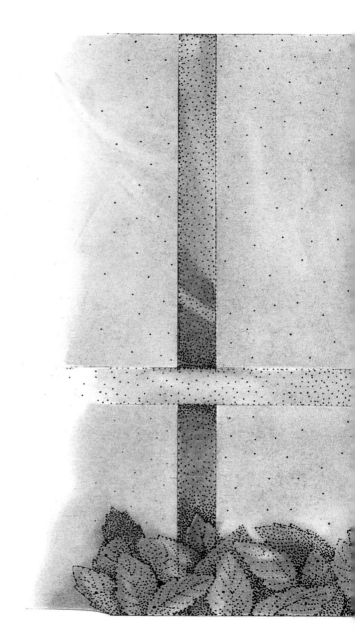

There was a rattle and a bang, and a great big wind blew out of the medicine bag.

It was louder than a taxi horn. It was louder than the wheels of a train.

The ghost wind blew and blew.

Thunder thundered, and the lightning lightninged! The magic flew right out of the medicine bag, and it blew the lock right off the door!

And so Thunderspirit set Nanabee the sheep free.

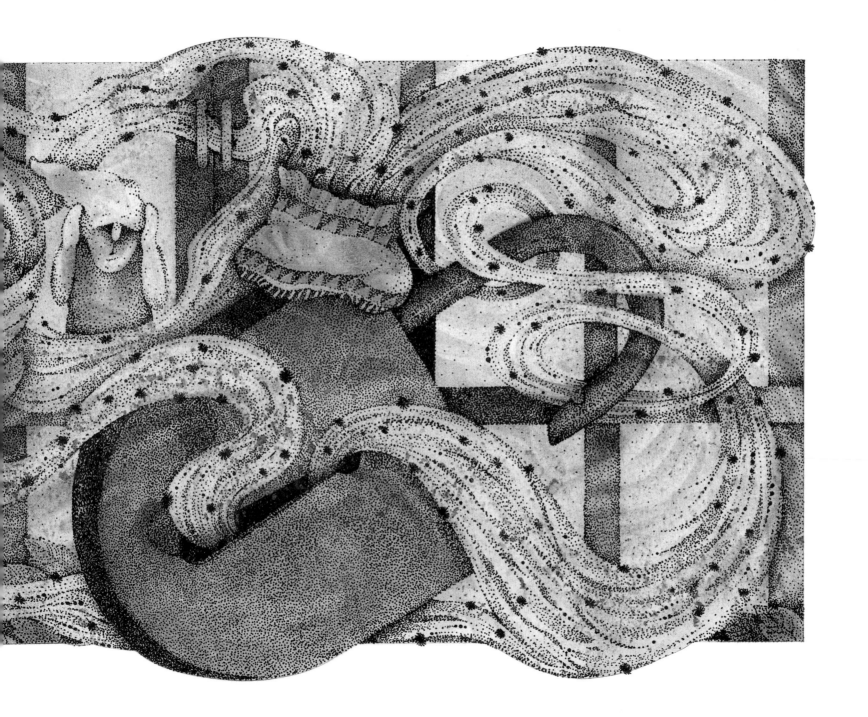

Then they went back to the park and found the Chief.

Thunderspirit told the Chief it was time to go back to the Pueblo again.

So all three of them went home.

And they were all happy to be back!

The Chief tried to think why he wanted to go to the city
in the first place.

Thunderspirit thought maybe it was so they could feel
good about not being there anymore.

But Nanabee didn't think anything. She had eaten too
much grass, and she was fast asleep.